Jesus,
HOW DO I KNOW IF
YOU'RE THERE?

Rebecca Kraemer

Cover design and illustrations by

Hardback ISBN-13:978-1-959213-02-4
Paperback ISBN-13: 978-1-959213-03-1
eBook ISBN-13:978-1-959213-10-9

Library of Congress Control Number: 2022915880

Kraemer, Rebecca

Jesus, How Do I know If You're There? /Rebecca Kraemer
Several animals in the forest are excited since Jesus had given them Jesus-ears to hear Him. They ask Jesus if they could get Jesus-eyes to see Him. Jesus asked them where they think He would put their Jesus eyes. After a discussion He told them He puts them In their heart. Jesus, How Do I Know If You're There? Encourages child-like faith and fellowship.

ISBN (hc) 978-1-959213-02-4

DEDICATION

This little book is dedicated to all of the parents who spend time with their kids, giving them hugs, baths, and vegetables! Those who cover them in prayer, hold them with their wiggles, and appreciate their giggles. You are my heroes!

In this day, it's a God-size challenge to make the time for these who are His special ones. I commend you. You are one of the few who do.

Special thanks to Donna Carr and Susan Arcadia. Although God started this journey by giving me this story, it was their expertise, love for me, and God's vision that completed it. I am but a very small part.

Mr. Frog

Hey, guys! My mind has been spinning today! It's just been a bit befuddled.

Mr. Turtle

Befuddled?

What's befuddled? Did you make that word up all by yourself? It's kind of a fun word. Maybe if I thought as much as you do, I could make fun words, too!

Mr. Frog

It may be a fun word but it leaves me perplexed. I've got a tough question that I just can't get settled! Maybe you can help? Here's what's got me stumped:

How can I be sure that Jesus is there if I can't see Him?

Mrs. Bird

Oh, what a silly question to ask. We don't have to see Him to know He's there. I hear Him whisper all the time—when I'm awake and when I'm asleep and dreaming. I hear Him when I'm happy, when I'm sad, even when I'm mad. Do I have to see Him like I see you? No, Mr. Frog! I sure don't have to! I know He's there even so.

Mr. Turtle

Oh, how I love my Jesus! I hear His whispers with my Jesus-ears and know He's always there! But how to see Him, I guess I don't know.

Miss Butterfly

That's not a silly question at all! It's hard to know if someone is there if we can't see or hear them. First, you have to believe He's there, then you have to ask! Jesus loves it when we ask Him questions. That's how I got my Jesus-ears, and Jesus-eyes too! Jesus said all I needed to do was ask, so I did. And BAM! Now I can see Him everywhere and I can hear Him whisper anytime!

Mr. Giraffe

You can? Wow! I can't think of anything better. I'm awfully tall—I'd probably always see where He is with Jesus-eyes. He'd never be able to hide from me!

Do you think He'd give me Jesus-eyes too? How much do they cost? I'd trade anything to get them. Would my long tail or my spots be enough?

Miss Butterfly

Well, you all know Jesus—His heart is so big. It seems He just waits to hear our voices so He can respond to us. Asking for my Jesus-eyes was really very simple.

I always knew Jesus was there. But with Jesus-eyes, I can see how big His love is! That's the way He meant it to be!

Mr. Frog

That sounds good, but give me some facts: what was the first thing you saw with your new Jesus-eyes? Did you see Him? Did things really change? Were you surprised?

Mrs. Bird

Oh, yes! I want to know too! What does He look like? Does He have a big nose, floppy ears, or even big toes?

Mr. Turtle

Hold it! Hold it! Slow down just a little. Our Jesus-ears aren't ears like the ones that stick to our heads. So we know that Jesus-eyes will be different too. We'll see more than the usual stuff.

This is exciting! These are Jesus-eyes! They're cooler than ours. Imagine what we'd see!

Miss Butterfly

It's hard to explain but I'm going to try.

The first thing I saw was His love and His care. It was everywhere!

I suddenly saw why He made the sky blue and all the flowers full of colors. He knows colors make me happy and He wants me happy. I saw why He gave me friends like you; it's because you make me feel loved and He wants me loved. I knew my wings weren't just for flying—I suddenly saw the design He made just for me. I love my Jesus-eyes!

Mr. Frog

I get it! I want them! How about the rest of you? Do you want them, too?

All

Yes! Yes! Yes!

Mr. Giraffe

Well, then… let's ask! Will you show us how to ask, Miss Butterfly?

Miss Butterfly

Of course! It's easy! He's always with us. We can talk to Him just like we're talking to each other now. Like this:

Hello, Jesus! It's us! We're all here! My friends have a question for You.

Mr. Giraffe

We all just love our Jesus-ears. Right guys?

But we've been talking with Miss Butterfly and are wondering… do You think... could You maybe… only if You really want to… give us Jesus-eyes, too? We'd love to see You!

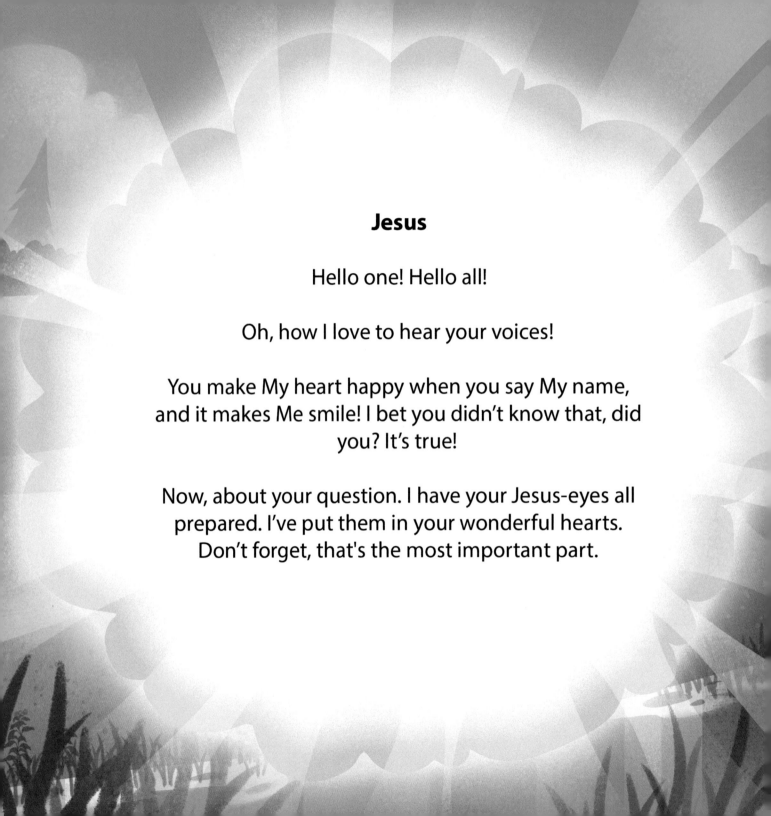

Jesus

Hello one! Hello all!

Oh, how I love to hear your voices!

You make My heart happy when you say My name, and it makes Me smile! I bet you didn't know that, did you? It's true!

Now, about your question. I have your Jesus-eyes all prepared. I've put them in your wonderful hearts. Don't forget, that's the most important part.

With them you'll see all My love gifts to you! We will have so much fun!

Oh, and Mr. Giraffe, I want you to keep your spots and your tail. They're your special love gifts from Me!

I want each of you to know and always remember that My gifts are yours forever and are totally free. I'm always here with you. That's the way I've meant for it to be.

Mr. Giraffe

Oh yes! I see differently now! Miss Butterfly, you're right! I know I have my Jesus-eyes because I even see myself differently! My long neck and silly spots used to make me feel weird, but now I see, Jesus… You made me special. You made me me. You're right here with me

Miss Bird

Oh, Jesus! Your Jesus-eyes are so different from mine! They do help my heart see You all around. Look! I can see Your kindness toward me! You know I love to fly high. You made my feathers so I can reach for the sky! You are always here with me!

Mr. Turtle

I'm usually slow to understand things. But Jesus, You make things so easy! Your Jesus-eyes make my heart see so clearly. I see You all around—in the shade of trees, in the warmth of the sun, and in the protection of my shell. No matter how slow I go, I see that You are always with me. And with my Jesus-ears, we can talk as I go!

Mr. Frog

Thank you, Miss Butterfly. I'm no longer befuddled! I can see clearly now! My Jesus-eyes give me eyes to see my brain in a whole new way. I sometimes bother others with all the things I think about. That brings up all kinds of questions. But it's the love of Jesus, you see, that made my brain—and then He gave it as His love gift to me. He wants me to ask questions! He loves to hear my voice! He has secrets He wants to tell me so I can tell others! He is always with me!

Miss Butterfly

See, dear friends, what a wonderful Jesus we have! He *IS* all around! We were never alone, even when we couldn't see Him. What adventures we will have together.

Goodbye, dear friend! Always remember to look for Jesus. You can color us any color you want. This is your page!

ABOUT THE AUTHOR

Rebecca is a 72-year-old who finds herself, after 50 wonderful years, a widow who is unexpectedly being redefined into "author." She is also a mother and grandmother. As a Christian for 45 years, she has had many God adventures, such as church planting, 10 years serving with Youth With A Mission around the world, and just as importantly, serving her community as a cardiac nurse.

Her grandchildren would say that she is not your typical "grandmother." She regularly enjoys manicures and pedicures and loves to try "un-grandma-like" colors! She has a fondness for unique clothes, going out for coffee with friends, fruits and vegetables, and prayer walks.

Dear Elizabeth,
Stay awesome!
Carol van Den Hende

CARC VAN DEN HENDE

Orchid Blooming

a novel

Azine Press™

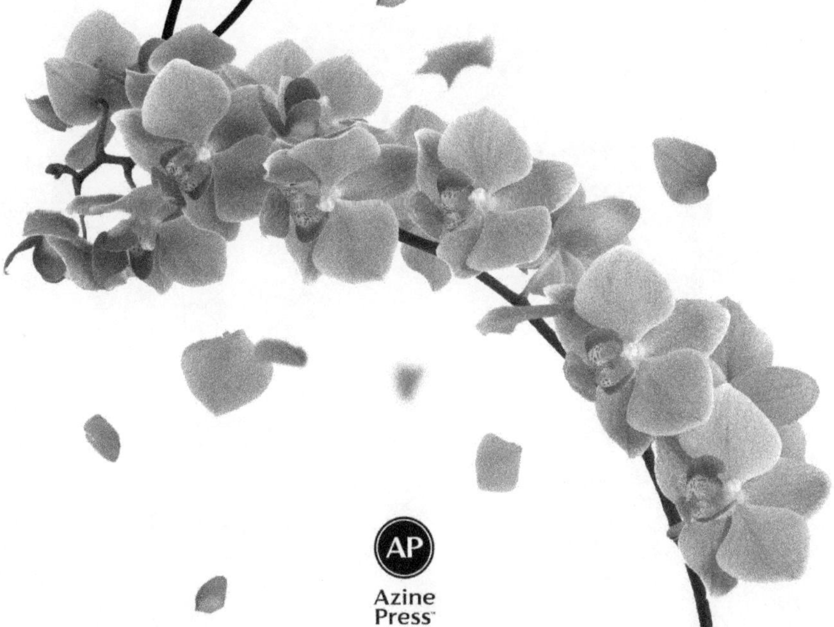

Dear Elizabeth,
Stay awesome!